For Zachary, who had my favorite missing tooth smile.

For all the kids who taught me in Room 24
at Cleburne County Elementary School.

And for my friend, Ralph Peterson, who helps us
remember the importance of celebrations.

—L.L.L.

Ω

Published by
PEACHTREE PUBLISHERS
1700 Chattahoochee Avenue
Atlanta, Georgia 30318-2112

www.peachtree-online.com

Text © 1998 by Lester L. Laminack
Illustrations © 1998 by Kathi Garry McCord

First trade paperback edition published in 2002

Manufactured in Singapore

10 9 8 7 6 5 (hardcover)
10 9 8 7 6 5 4 (trade paperback)

Library of Congress Cataloging-in-Publication Data
Laminack, Lester L., 1956-
   Trevor's wiggly-wobbly tooth / Lester L. Laminack; illustrated by
Kathi Garry McCord. -- 1st ed.
        p. cm.
   Summary: Although he is happy about having a loose tooth, Trevor worries
when his classmates tell him some of the ways others might try to
pull out the tooth.
   ISBN 13: 978-1-56145-175-3 / ISBN 10: 1-56145-175-4 (hardcover)
   ISBN 13: 978-1-56145-279-8 / ISBN 10: 1-56145-279-3 (trade paperback)
[1. Teeth—fiction. 2. Schools—fiction.] I. Garry McCord, Kathleen,
ill. II. Title.
PZ7.L1815Tr   1998
[E]—dc21
                                                    98-7210
                                                     CIP
                                                     AC

for Heidi,

Trevor's Wiggly-Wobbly Tooth

Lester L. Laminack

Illustrated by
Kathi Garry McCord

Lester Laminack 6/08

PEACHTREE
ATLANTA

Everyone in Mr. Thompson's first grade class had a missing tooth smile. Everyone except Trevor.

But on Monday, Trevor went to school with a wiggly tooth. He was so excited. He showed Tillman and C.J. how he could wiggle it with his finger.

"You should wiggle it all day so it will come out sooner," C.J. said.

"How are you going to pull it out?" Tillman asked.

C.J. smiled broadly so Trevor could see the little windows in his mouth. "You know, you could just pull it yourself. One big tug and it's out," he said.

"But," C.J. warned, "don't let anyone try to pull it out with a string on a door. When my tooth was loose, my Uncle Everett tied a string to it and tied the other end to the bedroom doorknob."

Trevor's eyes got big. Then he whispered, "Did it work?"

"I don't know," C.J. said. "I yanked the string off and hid under my bed."

Trevor began to worry.

After school, Trevor showed Tillman how he could wiggle his tooth just a little more.

"Oooh," Tillman said, "don't let your big sister know about it! My sister wanted to tie a string to my tooth. She was gonna tie the other end to her bike! She said she would pedal real fast and just snatch that tooth right out. I hid in my tree house forever just to keep her away."

Trevor bit his lip. Now he was really worried.

That evening, Trevor peered into the bathroom mirror with his mouth wide open. He was trying to see what his tooth looked like when he wiggled it.

His big sister was watching him and grinning. "You know," she said, reaching down deep in her pocket, "I could just pull it out quickly with this string…." Trevor didn't stay long enough to hear the rest of her plan.

"Don't worry," his mom said. "Just wait. That tooth will come out when it's ready." But Trevor wasn't taking any chances. He searched through all the kitchen drawers, rolling up pieces of string into a ball. He hid the ball in a shoe box in his closet.

On Tuesday, Trevor's tooth wiggled even more. Now he had a wiggly-wobbly tooth. Trevor showed C.J. and Tillman how his tooth wiggled and wobbled.

"Yep, Trevor, but don't let your big brother try to pull it. Brothers always want to pull a wiggly tooth," Tillman warned. "When my tooth was loose, my big brother tried to pull it with his fingers. He tried to pull it with a string. He even wanted to pull it with pliers, but my mom wouldn't let him."

Trevor wanted the tooth to come out. But he was not ready to have it *pulled* out. He especially didn't want anyone to try it with pliers! Trevor pressed his lips together as tightly as they would go. He was thinking about those big pliers in the tool box at home under the kitchen sink.

On Wednesday, Trevor could wiggle that tooth even more.

"Let me see," said Carmen. "Can you wiggle it with your tongue?" Carmen smiled. Her mouth was a big zigzag with missing teeth on top and growing-in teeth on the bottom. "Yup. You know it's gonna be soon when you can wiggle it with your tongue."

Trevor practiced all day wiggling the tooth with his tongue.

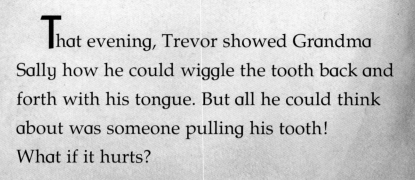

That evening, Trevor showed Grandma Sally how he could wiggle the tooth back and forth with his tongue. But all he could think about was someone pulling his tooth! What if it hurts?

YIKES!! … fingers … string … PLIERS!!

He wanted that tooth to come out, but he did *not* want to have someone *pull* it out.

"Just wait," his mother said. "That tooth will come out when it's ready."

Grandma Sally pinched his cheeks and made little clucking noises with her tongue. "Your mom is right. Those wiggly teeth pick their own time," she said with a wink.

Trevor wiggled the tooth furiously with his tongue.

On Thursday, Trevor wiggled his tooth with his fingers. He wiggled his tooth with his tongue. He wiggled his tooth all morning. He wiggled his tooth at lunch. He wiggled his tooth on the bus.

At home that afternoon, he was wiggling his tooth out and in, back and forth, when he heard a little pop. Now his tooth made a squishy sound when it wiggled. And the tip of his tongue could feel the rough edge on the bottom of that tooth.

His dad said, "I think that tooth is about ready to come out. Come on over here and let me just pull it out for you."

Trevor sat very still. He thought about what Tillman and C.J. had said about other people pulling your teeth. He thought about his dad's fingers pulling that tooth. He thought about the string he had hidden in his closet and about the pliers under the kitchen sink.

But his mom leaned over and smiled. "Don't worry, Trevor," she assured him. "Just wait. That tooth will come out when it's ready."

On Friday, Trevor went to school with a squishy, wiggly-wobbly tooth. But no one noticed because Grandma Sally went along, too. Grandma Sally had visited his first grade many times. And when she went to school something wonderful always happened.

Mr. Thompson explained, "Grandma Sally is going to make candy with the class today. She will show us how folks used to make taffy when she was a little girl. And we all get to help with the taffy pull."

When the taffy was made, everyone had a piece. Tillman bit into his taffy and pulled the other end. It stretched out a long way. Everyone laughed.

Then C.J. tried it. And Carmen did, too. When Trevor tried it, something funny happened. Carmen was the first to notice.

"Look, Trevor! Your tooth! It's in your taffy!" she said. Everyone looked. Sure enough, Trevor's squishy, wiggly-wobbly tooth was stuck in his taffy. Trevor opened his mouth wide with surprise. Then he felt the new hole with his tongue.

"Way to go, Trevor!" Mr. Thompson cheered. "Now everyone in the class is a member of the Missing Tooth Club," Mr. Thompson said as he gave Trevor a tiny treasure chest to keep his tooth in.

Trevor showed Grandma Sally his new missing tooth smile and held up the taffy so she could see the tooth stuck in it. "My tooth came out, Grandma Sally, and it didn't even hurt!"

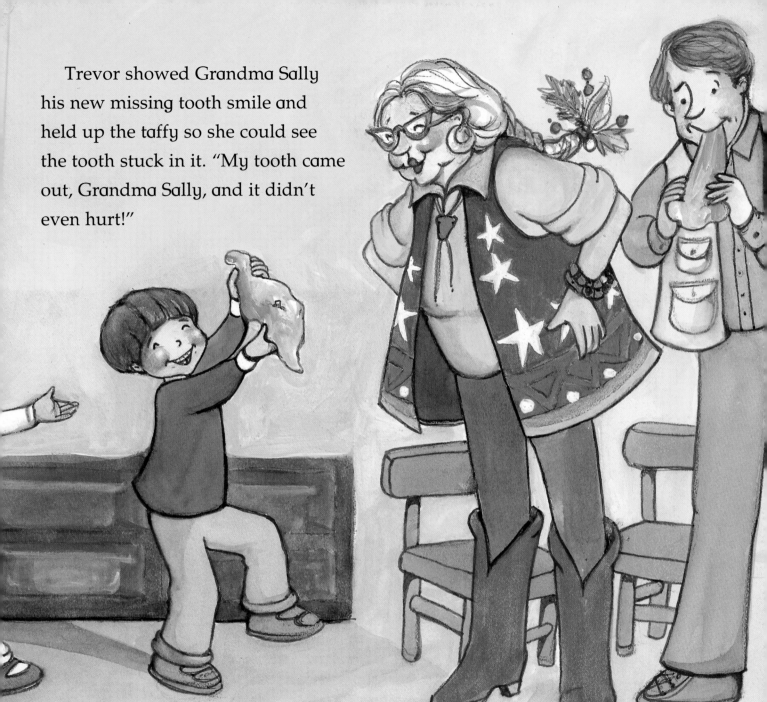

Grandma Sally gave Trevor a proud grandmother smile and reached over to the plate of taffy. She took the biggest piece, and Trevor watched as she sank her teeth into the chewy candy.

She gave Trevor a little wink and gave the taffy a big tug to stretch it out. But, when Grandma Sally did it, ALL of her top front teeth came out in the taffy!

Trevor burst out laughing. So did Grandma Sally and the rest of the class. Mr. Thompson laughed so hard his face turned red and his taffy popped out of his mouth.

Grandma Sally asked Mr. Thompson if he would take a picture of the Missing Tooth Club. Trevor and his classmates all gathered in the front of the room for the photo.

And there in the middle was Grandma Sally, with the biggest missing tooth smile of all!

And Trevor? Well, on Monday Trevor went to school with a missing tooth smile, two shiny quarters, and his wiggly-wobbly tooth in the tiny treasure chest.